Praise for Storyshares

"One of the brightest innovators and game-changers in the education industry."
— Forbes

"Your success in applying research-validated practices to promote literacy serves as a valuable model for other organizations seeking to create evidence-based literacy programs." — Library of Congress

"We need powerful social and educational innovation, and Storyshares is breaking new ground. The organization addresses critical problems facing our students and teachers. I am excited about the strategies it brings to the collective work of making sure every student has an equal chance in life."
— Teach For America

"It's the perfect idea. There's really nothing like this. I mean, wow, this will be a wonderful experience for young people." — Andrea Davis Pinkney, Executive Director, Scholastic

"Reading for meaning opens opportunities for a lifetime of learning. Providing emerging readers with engaging texts that are designed to offer both challenges and support for each individual will improve their lives for years to come. Storyshares is a wonderful start."
— David Rose, Co-founder of CAST & UDL

Storyshares presents

Published by Storyshares, LLC

Storyshares
Storyshares, LLC
24 N. Bryn Mawr Avenue #340
Bryn Mawr, Pennsylvania 19010-3304
www.storyshares.org

Inspiring reading with a new kind of book.

Interest Level: High School
Grade Level Equivalent: 4.2

ISBN 9798885977791
Book design by Saskia Globig

BURGUNDY SKIES

Piper Arington

Storyshares

CONTENTS

CHAPTER ONE

All Jacob wanted was sleep. Just barely returned from the night watch, he'd not even had a chance to sit on his bed.

"C'mon boys, you know what today is!"

He heard Mother call from the front room.

Sighing raggedly, Jacob turned from the temptation of his bed. He grabbed a jacket and stumbled toward the living space.

The others had already gathered around the table, except for Brother.

Fumbling tiredly with his zipper, he managed to get the jacket on his shoulders correctly.

"Good morning, Son. Have you heard from Brother yet?" Mother asked as she grabbed breakfast from the shelves.

"I haven't seen him since he left the Hill last night, Mother. Not surprised he slept in, though."

The last part he mumbled mostly to himself. Keeping an eye on Sister, who was tottering slightly too close to the fire, Jacob walked toward Brother's room.

A slight chuckle left his mouth at the sight of Brother. The man was well over six feet tall. He was hanging half over the side of his bed.

Drool was dribbling from the side of his mouth onto his blanket.

Quietly Jacob slipped over to the side of the bed. Taking a deep breath, Jacob took a hold of the bed and heaved as hard as he could.

With a yelp and a thunderous crash, Brother sprawled across the floor.

The look of bewilderment on his face was too much for Jacob. He clutched his sides as laughter spilled from his mouth.

Brother was still trying to gather his wits. He looked at Jacob, then the bed, then back to Jacob. He slowly started to scowl.

"Asshole," Brother sneered as he shakily got to his feet, fixing his tattered shorts and scarf.

CHAPTER TWO

"Your fault for sleeping past dawn," Jacob answered.

He walked back toward the group. "It's the first of Mid-Season today," he casually threw over his shoulder.

The slight choking sound from behind him was Brother's only response.

When dawn had risen over the Hill this morning, Jacob had already been preparing his pack. Then he was able to settle down and watch the muddy, burgundy clouds out his single window.

He knew that Brother wouldn't have even looked at his pack yet, let alone started preparing.

Returning to the dining area, Jacob scooped Sister up from her perch near the fire and tossed her into the air.

Her joyous giggling brought a soft smile to his lips. But his smile was touched with a hint of melancholy, making him slightly sad.

At only three years old, this life was the only one Sister had known. He couldn't decide if that made her luckier than the rest of them or not.

Mother started arranging their bowls into a circle at the table. Across the room, Grandfather slowly rose from his seat.

The patriarch of their group and the eldest was remarkably fit at eighty-two. Still, Jacob could not help but cringe at the slight limp in Grandfather's leg as he walked to the table.

Sister squirmed in Jacob's arms, so he set her down. She ran to sit beside Grandfather.

Mother smiled at the pair as they began to whisper between themselves.

No one could quite explain the bond between these two. Perhaps it was that they were the last to join and at roughly the same time.

"I pray for the day I never have to see one of these monstrosities again," Grandfather cursed as he tore open the plastic coating around those godforsaken sweets and handed it to the toddler beside him.

Sister took the treat and began happily munching. Grandfather was less enthusiastic, but nevertheless took a bite.

Mother carefully poured the dry oatmeal into everyone's bowl, only a third of a packet for each person.

CHAPTER THREE

Brother made his way to the table and sat down with a huff.

Glaring down at the small bit of dry oatmeal and sugar wrapped in cellophane, he turned to Mother. "Why so little? We can't be that low on supplies?"

Mother just shrugged her shoulders in explanation.

She turned to settle down next to Sister as Brother continued to glare.

Jacob couldn't help the flare of protectiveness that consumed him. He hated when Brother looked at Mother like everything was her fault. She was doing her best. That's all any of them were doing.

They settled at the table and tucked into their meager breakfasts.

"I think Mother should stay behind with Sister and Grandfather today," Jacob said, picking at his oatmeal.

Mother, who was wiping Sister's face, froze and turned to look at him. Brother slowly started to grin.

Mother wiped the last bit of frosting from Sister's face and turned to him. "Why? You know it's safer in groups."

"I know, I just worry about Grandfather all alone here with Sister for such a long time."

He glanced at Brother, meeting his dark eyes and urging him to stay quiet.

"It's not more than a few hours. They will be fine," Mother argued.

"It's taking longer with every Mid-Season and you know it," Jacob answered her. "It took us nearly seven hours last time.

"What happens when it takes thirteen this time, or twenty? It's getting harder and harder to find usable materials. Not to mention more dangerous," Jacob added.

"It's not fair to expect Grandfather to watch Sister that long. And what about when something happens to all three of us when we are out?" he finished, crossing his arms and staring her down.

"Nothing is going to happen!" Mother was casting anxious glances at Sister.

"You can't know that!"

CHAPTER FOUR

"Well, you don't know that all three of us are going to be somehow compromised at the same time!"

Mother's face was turning red. If he couldn't convince her soon, she would only insist on going with them out of spite.

Luckily, Grandfather chose that moment to speak up.

"I... hate to agree with Grandson. But I would feel much more comfortable if another person was here. I'm not the young man I used to be. Granddaughter is a joy to be with, but she has a lot of energy for me to handle for such a long time."

He looked sorry while he said it. He was apologizing to Mother with his eyes already.

Mother stood from the table and looked at all of them. Then she turned to think.

Her shoulders were bunched high up by her ears. They betrayed her anxiety over the situation.

Jacob felt bad for pushing her about this, but it was the safest compromise he could come up with.

Mother was quietly muttering to herself now. Brother's leg was shaking beside him. He was anxiously awaiting her response.

As much as they did not get along, Brother always left the final decision to Mother.

Jacob also thought Brother was hoping to find maternal comfort. It was a shame he was too unwilling to trust. Maybe Mother could have truly helped him.

Mother turned back around again and evaluated the whole group. Sister was wriggling in her seat, eager to get back to her toys on the floor.

Grandfather was trying to get her to stay and eat just a little bit more.

Mother's face turned more conflicted. The corners of her mouth drew down and her brow furrowed heavily.

Jacob stood and approached her. He took her shoulders in his hands and pulled her into a hug.

"Brother and I were doing this for over a year

before you found us. It's second nature at this point," he said.

She huffed and slapped his shoulder.

Her eyes were welled with tears when she looked up at him.

CHAPTER FIVE

"It shouldn't have to be second nature," she sniffed. "You boys are too young to have that kind of pressure on your shoulders."

"The world doesn't stop so we can all have the perfect childhood, Mother. Everyone had to make do when the storms started, regardless of their age."

He pulled her head to his shoulder and hugged her tightly once again.

"Brother and I will be more than fine. Use today to start carving out the new room for Sister. We're behind on that, anyway."

Mother pulled away and met his gaze.

"I don't like it. But I understand the logic."

She turned to Brother sitting at the table. He was reaching for the rest of Jacob's oatmeal.

"I expect you to listen to your brother the entire time you are out there. I don't care who is older; you're far too reckless on your own."

Brother just smiled lazily back at her. "I wouldn't dream of disobeying the chosen one, Mother. Don't worry."

She clicked her tongue at his cheek but let it slide.

Grandfather looked at Mother before turning to Jacob. He considered him for a moment, then offered a slight nod of thanks. Then he turned back to help clean up Sister.

Mother walked over to the stool on the far side of the room. She dragged it over to the small opening above the fire pit.

She slowly climbed the three small steps. She removed the brick used to trap in the heat.

Her head turned from side to side for a few moments. Then she nodded to herself and came back down the steps.

"You've got about ten minutes before Break One starts," she announced.

CHAPTER SIX

Brother quickly stood from the table and rushed to his pack. He was frantically checking things over, adding, removing, reconsidering, and then re-adding things to the bag.

He always did this.

Brother always seemed to think the closer to leaving he packed, the less likely something was to go missing from his pack.

The logic was flawed, but no one had been able to convince him otherwise. Or to break him of the habit.

While Brother was going through his pack, Jacob turned to retrieve his own from his room.

Mother stopped him along the way. "Take my two bottles as well. Split them between you and your brother. I don't trust him to hold the extra on his own. He'll just waste it," she whispered.

She slid the two pint-sized bottles of water into his hands.

Jacob softly nodded his head and went to add them to his own bag. In the comfort of his own space, he checked his pack one last time. Water, rope, flint stone, knife, and three empty bottles.

Securing the ties, he turned to look out the window again.

The clouds were still their normal rust color, but he could start to see the break to the blue open sky.

It would be there soon.

About five minutes until Break One.

Then approximately fifty-two minutes to get to Base Two before the deluge of poison came again.

Brother found him two minutes later, retying his shoes for the fourth time.

"Ready?" he asked, his pack slung over his shoulder.

"As I'll ever be," Jacob replied. He lifted his own bag onto his back.

CHAPTER SEVEN

The two walked back to the front room. Mother was waiting by the hatch. She had both three-gallon containers sitting at her feet.

Brother picked one and attached it to the bottom of his pack. Jacob did the same.

Mother looked on with worried eyes.

Grandfather was watching out the small window.

Mother hugged Brother and then Jacob. Then she stepped back to allow them space to move.

Picking up Sister, she pointed back at them and urged her to wave goodbye.

Brother chuckled and waved back.

Jacob sent a small smile to Sister and a reassuring look to Mother.

"Get ready," Grandfather said.

He and Brother each put a hand on the steel hatch door. They both turned and braced their shoulders along the side beams.

Brother's breathing accelerated. He looked at Jacob with a mix of excitement and fear.

"No retreats," Brother said, sticking his free hand out.

"Or hesitation," Jacob responded, grasping Brother's hand tightly in his own.

They locked eyes and waited for the signal.

Grandfather began the countdown. "Three..."

Mother was counting on them. So were Grandfather and Sister. Any fights or childish ribbing were put aside.

"Two..."

Outside this home was the world at its most cruel. This was survival in the very basest of terms.

"One..."

He and Brother had no one outside these walls but each other and their ability to endure. No retreats or hesitation.

"Go!"

About the Author

Piper lives in a small apartment with her family and two adorable cats, Gatito and George. She tries to go to the forests as often as she can so the faeries and sprites can whisper their stories in her ear. A lifelong fan of fantasy and magic, this story is her first endeavor into a post apocalyptic world!

About the Publisher

Storyshares is a publisher focused on supporting the millions of teens and adults who struggle with reading by creating a new shelf in the library specifically for them. The ever-growing collection features content that is compelling and culturally relevant for teens and adults, yet still readable at a range of lower reading levels.

Storyshares generates content by engaging deeply with writers, bringing together a community to create this new kind of book. With more intriguing and approachable stories to choose from, the teens and adults who have fallen behind are improving their skills and beginning to discover the joy of reading.

For more information, visit storyshares.org.

Easy to Read. Hard to Put Down.